Biscuit
Finds a Friend

Biscuit
Finds a Friend

story by Alyssa Satin Capucilli

pictures by Pat Schories

SCHOLASTIC INC.

New York   Toronto   London   Auckland   Sydney
Mexico City   New Delhi   Hong Kong   Buenos Aires

ISBN 0-439-65034-8

Text copyright © 1997 by Alyssa Satin Capucilli.
Illustrations copyright © 1997 by Pat Schories. All rights reserved.
Published by Scholastic Inc., 557 Broadway, New York, NY 10012,
by arrangement with HarperCollins Publishers.
SCHOLASTIC and associated logos are trademarks and/or
registered trademarks of Scholastic Inc.

50 49 48 47 46   21 22 23 24/0

Printed in the U.S.A.   40

First Scholastic printing, February 2004

I Can Read Book® is a trademark of HarperCollins Publishers Inc.

For two very special friends,
Margaret Jean O'Connor and Willie Hornick.

Woof! Woof!

What has Biscuit found?

Is it a ball?

Woof!

Is it a bone?

Woof!

Quack!

It is a little duck.

The little duck is lost.
Woof! Woof!

We will bring
the little duck
back to the pond.

Woof! Woof!

Here, little duck.

Here is the pond.

Here are your mother
and your father.
Quack!

Here are your brothers
and your sisters.
Quack! Quack!

The ducks say thank you.
Thank you for finding
the little duck.

Quack!
The little duck
wants to play.

Quack!
Woof!

Quack!
Woof!

17

Splash!

Biscuit fell into the pond!

Silly Biscuit.

You are all wet!

Woof!

Oh no, Biscuit.

Not a big shake!

Woof!

Time to go home, Biscuit.

Quack! Quack!

Say good-bye, Biscuit.

Woof! Woof!

Good-bye, little duck.

Biscuit has found
a new friend.